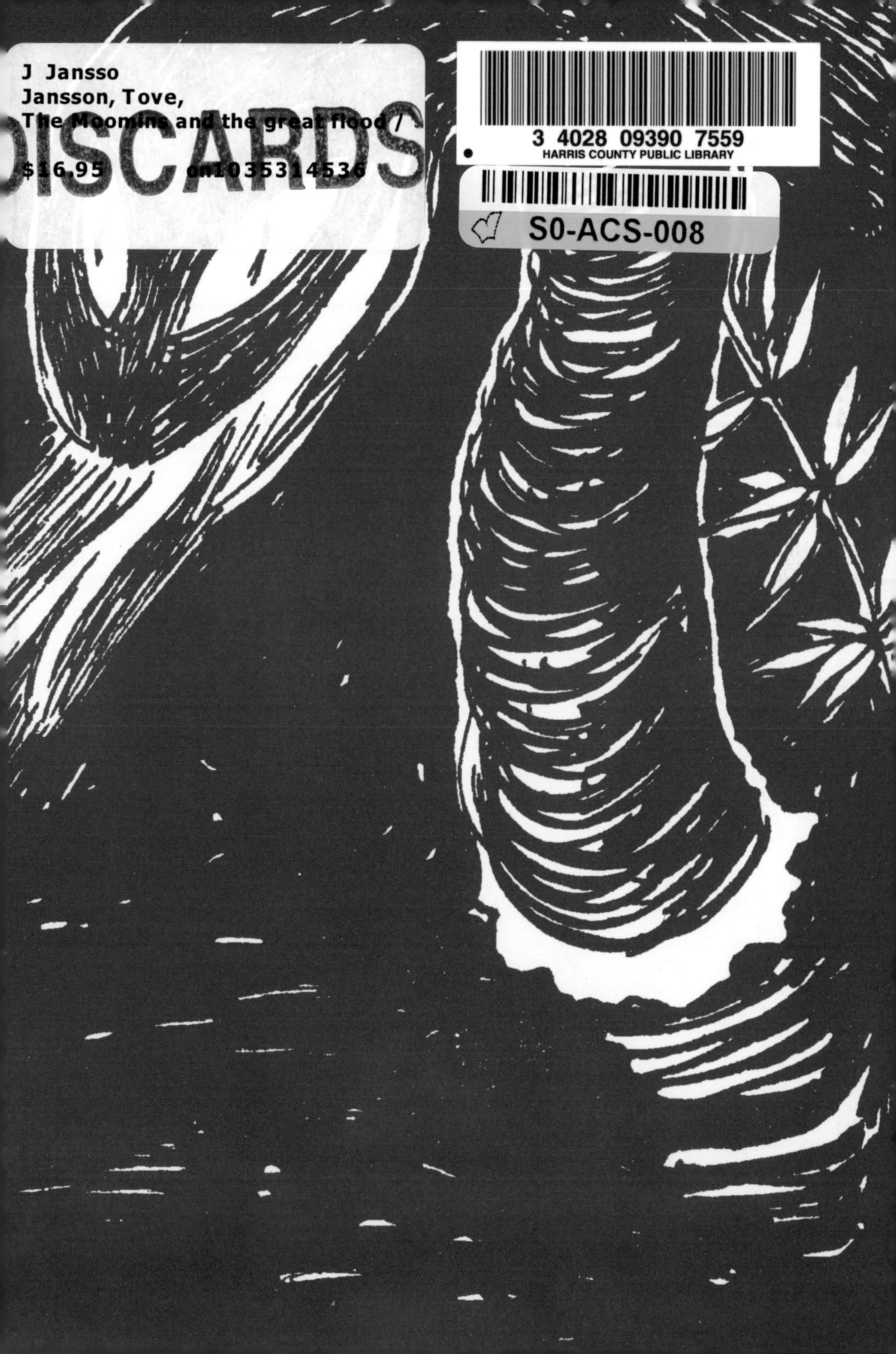

THE MOOMINS
AND THE GREAT FLOOD

TOVE JANSSON
Translated by David McDuff

ENFANT

drawnandquarterly.com

978-1-77046-328-8
First Drawn & Quarterly edition: July 2018
Printed in China
10 9 8 7 6 5 4 3 2 1

Cataloguing data available from Library and Archives Canada

Published in the USA by Drawn & Quarterly, a client publisher of Farrar, Straus and Giroux. Orders: 888.330.8477. Published in Canada by Drawn & Quarterly, a client publisher of Raincoast Books. Orders: 800.663.5714

The Moomins and the Great Flood was the first ever Moomin book, originally published in Finland in 1945.

Tove Jansson wrote the following preface when the story was reprinted in Scandinavia in 1991 after being out of print for many years.

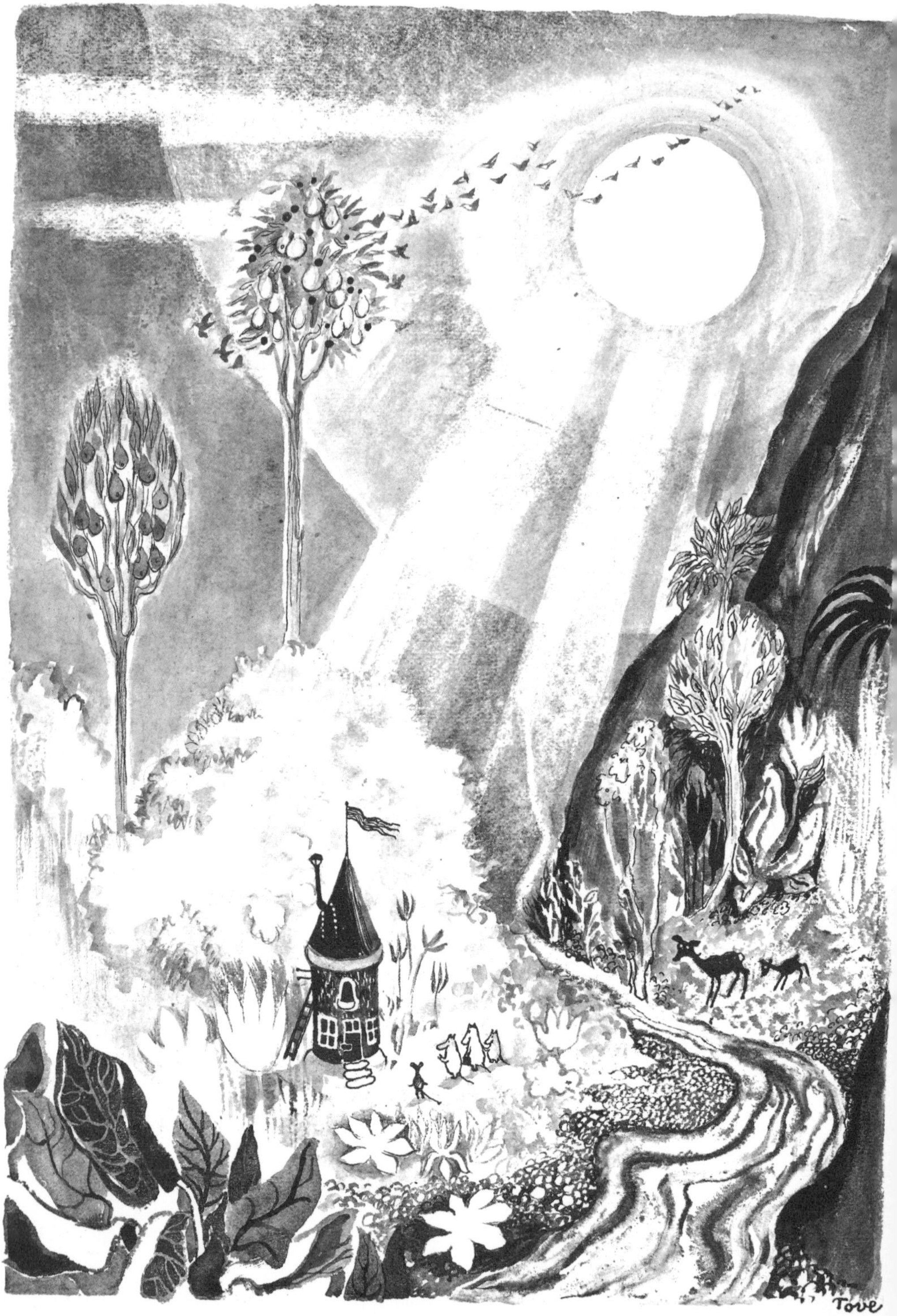
Tove

It was the winter of war, in 1939. One's work stood still; it felt completely pointless to try to create pictures.

Perhaps it was understandable that I suddenly felt an urge to write down something that was to begin with "Once upon a time."

What followed had to be a fairytale—that was inevitable—but I excused myself with avoiding princes, princesses, and small children and chose instead my angry signature character from the cartoons and called him the Moomintroll.

The half-written story was forgotten until 1945. Then a friend pointed out that it could become a children's book; just finish it and illustrate it; maybe they will want it.

I had thought that the title should connect to the Moomintroll and his search for his father—in the style of the search for Captain Grant—but the publisher wanted to make it easier for the readers by calling it *Småtrollen och den stora översvämningen* (*The Little Trolls and the Great Flood*).

The story is quite influenced by the childhood books I had read and loved, a bit of Jules Verne, some Collodi (the girl with the blue hair), and so on. But why not?

Anyhow, here was my very first happy ending!

Tove Jansson

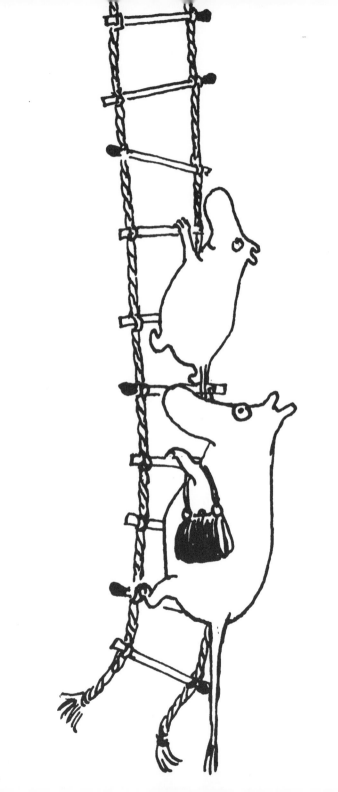

THE MOOMINS
AND THE GREAT FLOOD

I t must have been late in the afternoon one day at the end
of August when Moomintroll and his mother arrived at
the deepest part of the great forest. It was completely quiet,
and so dim between the trees that it was as though twilight had
already fallen. Here and there giant flowers grew, glowing with
a peculiar light like flickering lamps, and furthest in among the
shadows moved tiny dots of cold green.

"Glow-worms," said Moominmamma, but they had no time
to stop and take a closer look at them. They were out searching
for a snug, warm place where they could build a house to crawl
into when winter came. Moomins cannot stand the cold at all,
so the house would have to be ready by October at the latest.

So they walked on, further and further into the silence and
the darkness. Little by little, Moomintroll began to feel anxious,
and he asked his mother in a whisper if she thought there were
any dangerous creatures in there. "I shouldn't think so," she
said, "though perhaps we'd better go a little faster anyway. But
I hope we're so small that we won't be noticed if something
dangerous should come along."

13

Suddenly Moomintroll gripped his mother tightly by the arm. "Look!" he said, so frightened that his tail stuck straight out. From the shadows behind a tree-trunk, two eyes were staring at them.

At first Moominmamma was frightened too, but then she said soothingly: "It's really a very little creature. Wait, and I'll shine a light on it. Everything looks worse in the dark, you know."

And so she picked one of the big glowing flowers and lit up the shadows with it. Then they saw that there really was a very little creature sitting there, and that it looked friendly and a little scared. "There, you see," said Moominmamma.

"What sort of thing are you?" asked the little creature.

"I'm a moomintroll," answered Moomintroll, who had had time to feel brave again. "And this is my mother. I hope we didn't disturb you." (You can see that his mother had taught him to be polite.)

"Not at all," said the little creature. "I was sitting here feeling rather sad and longing for company. Are you in a big hurry?"

"Yes," said Moominmamma. "You see, we're looking for a nice, sunny place where we can build a house. But perhaps you'd like to come with us?"

"And how!" said the little creature, leaping out towards them. "I'd got lost and thought I'd never see the sun again!"

So all three continued, taking a large tulip with them to light the way. But around them the darkness thicken-ed all the time, the flowers glow-ed more faint-ly beneath the trees, and final-ly the very last one went out. In front of them gleamed a black stretch of water, and the air was heavy and cold.

15

"Oo, how horrid," said the little creature. "That's the swamp. I don't dare go there."

"Why not?" asked Moominmamma.

"Because that's where the Great Serpent lives," said the little creature in a very low voice, looking about him in all directions.

"Pooh!" said Moomintroll, wanting to show how brave he was. "We are so small that we wouldn't be noticed. How will we ever find the sunshine if we don't dare cross it? Just come along with us."

"Perhaps a bit of the way," said the little creature. "But be careful. On your own heads be it!"

So they took long strides as quietly as they could from tussock to tussock. The black mud bubbled and whispered all around them, but as long as the tulip lamp burned they felt calm. At one point, Moomintroll slipped and nearly fell in, but his mother caught hold of him at the last moment.

"We shall have to go on by boat," she said. "Now your feet are soaked. You're sure to catch cold." Then she got out a pair of dry socks for him from her handbag, and lifted him and the little creature up onto a big, round water-lily leaf. They all three stuck their tails in the water as paddles and then they steered straight out into the swamp. Beneath them they glimpsed dark creatures that swam in and out between the roots of the trees, there were splashing and diving sounds, and the mist came stealing over them. Suddenly the little creature said: "I want to go home now!"

"Don't be scared, little creature," said Moomintroll in a quavering voice. "We'll sing something cheerful and..."

At that very moment their tulip went out and it was completely dark. And out of the darkness they heard a hissing, and felt the water-lily leaf bobbing up and down. "Quick, quick!" cried Moominmamma. "The Great Serpent is coming!"

They stuck their tails in deeper, and paddled with all their might so that the water gushed around the bows. Now they could see the Serpent swimming up behind them. It looked wicked, and its eyes were cruel and yellow.

They paddled as hard as they could, but it kept gaining on them, and was already opening its mouth, with its long, flickering tongue. Moomintroll put his hands in front of his eyes and cried: "Mamma!" and then he waited to be eaten up.

But nothing happened. Then he looked cautiously between his fingers. Something very remarkable had happened. Their tulip was glowing again: it had opened all of its petals and in their midst stood a girl with bright blue hair reaching right down to her feet.

Brighter and brighter glowed the tulip. The Serpent began to blink, and suddenly it turned right round with an angry hiss and slid down into the mud.

Moomintroll, his mother and the little creature were so agitated and surprised that for a long time they couldn't say a word.

At last Moominmamma said solemnly: "Thank you so very much for your help, lovely lady." And Moomintroll bowed more deeply than he had ever done before, for the blue-haired girl was the most beautiful thing he had seen in all his life.

"Were you inside the tulip the entire time?" asked the little creature shyly. "It's my house," she said. "You may call me Tulippa."

And so they paddled slowly over to the other side of the swamp. Here the ferns were thick, and beneath them Moominmamma made a nest in the moss for them to sleep in. Moomintroll lay close beside his mother, listening to the song of the frogs out in the swamp. The night was full of strange, desolate sounds, and it was a long time before he fell asleep.

The next morning Tulippa led the way in front of them, and her blue hair shone like the brightest daylight lamp. The path climbed steeper and steeper, and at last the mountain rose straight up, so high that they could not see where it ended. "I expect there's sunshine up there," the little creature said, longingly. "I'm so dreadfully cold."

"Me too," said Moomintroll. And then he sneezed.

"What did I tell you?" said his mother. "Now you've got a cold. Please sit here while I make a fire." And then she gathered together an enormous heap of dry branches and lit it with

a spark from Tulippa's blue hair. They sat, all four of them, looking into the fire while Moominmamma told them stories. She told them about what it was like when she was young, when moomintrolls did not need to travel through fearsome forests and swamps in order to find a place to live in.

In those days they lived together with the house-trolls in people's houses, mostly behind their tall stoves. "Some of us still live there now, I'm sure," said Moominmamma. "But only where people still have stoves, I mean. We're not happy with central heating."

"Did the people know we were there?" asked Moomintroll.

"Some did," said his mother. "They felt us mostly as a cold draught on the back of their necks sometimes—when they were alone."

"Tell us something about Moominpappa," asked Moomintroll.

"He was an unusual moomintroll," said his mother, thoughtfully and sadly. "He was always wanting to move, from one stove to the next. He was never happy where he was. And then he disappeared—took off with the Hattifatteners, the little wanderers."

"What sort of folk are they?" asked the little creature.

"A kind of little troll-creature," explained Moominmamma. "They're mostly invisible. Sometimes they can be found under people's floors, and you can hear them pattering about in there when

it's quiet in the evenings. But mostly they wander round the world, don't stay anywhere, and don't care about anything. You can never tell if a Hattifattener is happy or angry, sad or surprised. I am sure that they have no feelings at all."

"And has Moominpappa become a Hattifattener now?" asked Moomintroll.

"No, of course not!" said his mother. "Surely you realize that they simply tricked him into going along with them."

"Imagine if we were to meet him one day!" said Tulippa. "He'd be pleased, wouldn't he?"

"Of course," said Moominmamma. "But I don't expect we shall." And then she cried. It sounded so sad that they all began to sob, and as they cried they began to think about a lot of other things that were sad, too, and that made them cry more and more. Tulippa's hair turned pale with sorrow and lost all its shine. When they had gone on like this for a good while, a stern voice suddenly rang out, saying: "What are you howling for down there?" They stopped at once and looked around them in all directions, but could not discover who was talking to them.

At the same time a rope-ladder came dangling down the rock face. High up, an old gentleman stuck his head out through a door in the mountain. "Well?" he shouted.

"Excuse me," said Tulippa, curtseying. "But you see, sir, it's really all very sad. Moominpappa has disappeared, and we're freezing and can't get over this mountain to find the sunshine, and we haven't anywhere to live."

"I see," said the old gentleman. "You'd better come up to my place, then. My sunshine is the finest you could imagine."

It was quite hard to climb up the rope-ladder, especially for Moomintroll and his mother, as they had such short legs. "Now you must wipe your feet," said the old gentleman, and drew the ladder up after them. Then he closed the door very carefully, so that nothing harmful could sneak inside. They all went up an escalator that carried them right inside the mountain.

"Are you sure this gentleman is to be trusted?" whispered the little creature. "Remember, on your own heads be it." And then he made himself as small as he could and hid behind Moominmamma. Then a bright light shone towards them, and the escalator took them straight into a wonderful landscape.

The trees sparkled with colour and were full of fruits and flowers they had never seen before, and below them in the grass lay gleaming white snowflakes. "Hurrah!" cried Moomintroll, and ran out to make a snowball.

"Be careful, it's cold!" called his mother. But when he ran his hands through the snow he noticed that it was not snow at all, but ice cream. And the green grass that gave way under his feet

was made of fine-spun sugar. Crisscross over the meadows ran brooks of every colour, foaming and bubbling over the golden sand. "Green lemonade!" cried the little creature, who had stooped down to drink. "It's not water at all, it's lemonade!" Moominmamma went straight over to a brook that was completely white, since she had always been very fond of milk. (Most moomintrolls are, at least when they get a bit older.) Tulippa ran from tree to tree picking armfuls of chocolates and sweets, and as soon as she had plucked one of the shining fruits, another grew at once.

They forgot their sorrows and ran further and further into the enchanted garden. The old gentleman slowly followed them and seemed very pleased by their wonder and admiration. "I made all this myself," he said. "The sun, too." And when they looked at the sun, they noticed that it really was not the real sun but a big lamp with fringes of gold paper.

"I see," said the little creature, with disappointment. "I thought it was the real sun. Now I can see that it has a slightly peculiar light."

"Well, that was the best I could do," said the old gentleman, offended. "But you like the garden, don't you?"

"Oh, yes," said Moomintroll, whose mouth was full of pebbles just then. (They were actually made of marzipan.) "If you would like to stay here, I will build you a candy house to live in," said the old gentleman. "I get a bit bored here sometimes all on my own."

"That would be very nice," said Moominmamma, "but if you don't mind, we must really be on our way. We were thinking of building a house in the real sunshine, you see."

"No, let's stay!" cried Moomintroll, the little creature, and Tulippa. "Well, children," said Moominmamma. "Wait and see." And she lay down to sleep under a chocolate bush.

When she woke up again she heard a fearful groaning, and realized at once that it was her Moomintroll, who had a tummy ache. (Moomins get tummy aches very easily.) It had become quite round from all he had eaten, and it hurt dreadfully. Beside him sat the little creature, who had goten a toothache from all the sweets, and was moaning even worse. Moominmamma did not scold, but took two powders from her handbag and gave them one each, and then she asked the old gentleman if he didn't have a pool of nice, hot porridge.

"No, I'm afraid not," he said. "But there's one of whipped cream, and another one of jam."

"Hm," said Moominmamma. "You can see for yourself that it's proper hot food they need. Where's Tulippa?"

"She says she can't get to sleep because the sun never goes down," said the old gentleman, looking unhappy. "I'm truly sorry that you don't like it here."

"We'll come back again," Moominmamma consoled him. "But now I really must see to it that we get out in the fresh air again." And so she took Moomintroll by one hand, and the little creature by the other, and called to Tulippa.

"You'll do best to take the switchback railway," said the old gentleman politely. "It goes right through the mountain and comes out in the middle of the sunshine."

"Thank you," said Moominmamma. "Goodbye then."

"Goodbye then," said Tulippa. (Moomintroll and the little creature were not able to say anything, as they felt so horribly sick.)

"Don't mention it," said the old gentleman.

And then they took the switchback railway through the whole mountain at a dizzying speed. When they came out on the other side they were quite giddy and sat on the ground for a long time, recovering. Then they looked around.

Before them lay the ocean, glittering in the sunshine. "I want to go for a swim!" cried Moomintroll, for now he felt all right again. "Me too," said the little creature, and so they ran

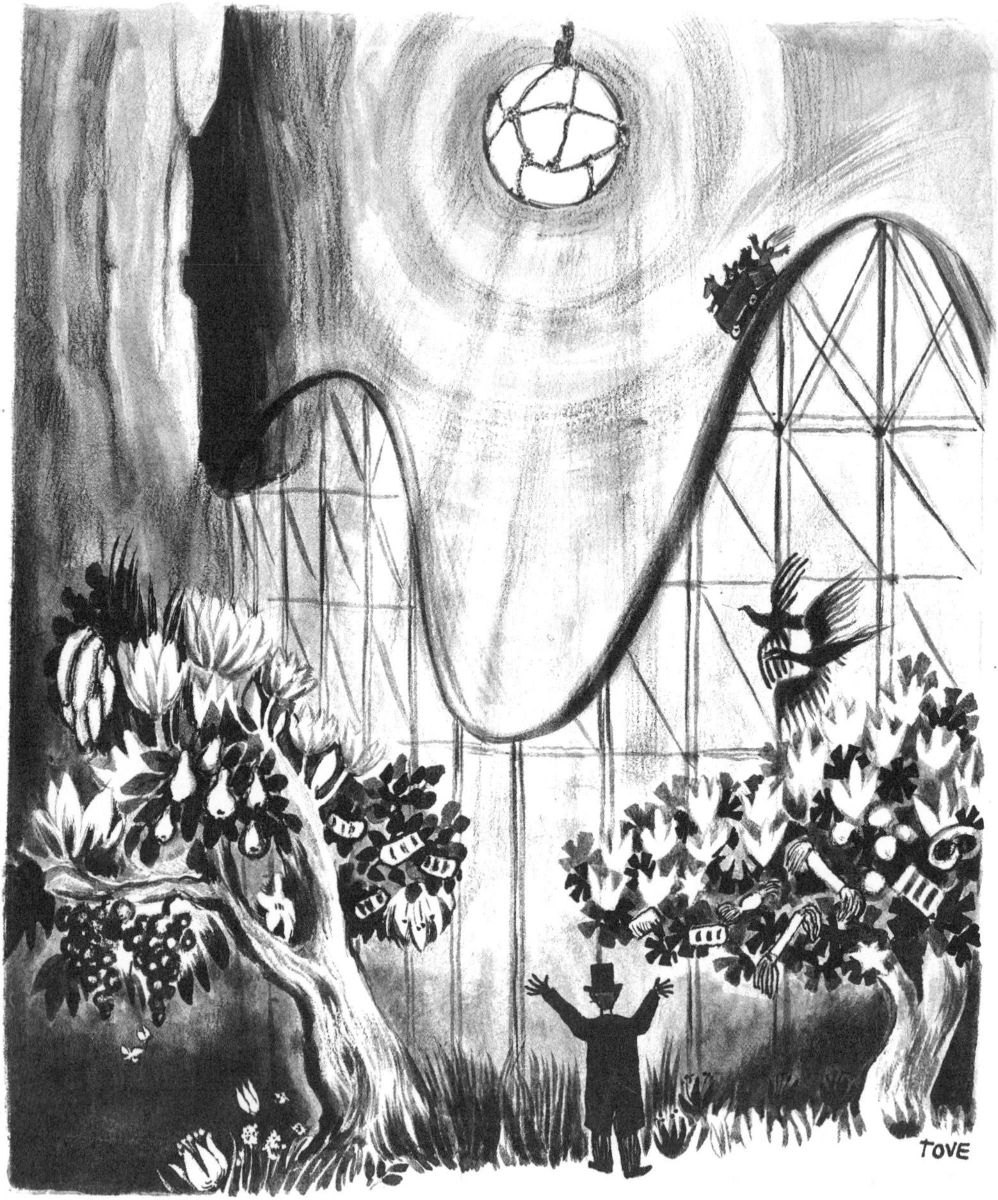
TOVE

right out into the sunbeam on the water.
Tulippa tied her hair up so it would not
go out, and then she followed them
and stepped in very cautiously.

"Ugh, it's so cold," she said.

"Don't stay in too long,"
called Moominmamma, and
then she lay down to sunbathe,
for she was still quite tired.

All at once an ant-lion came
strolling across the sand. He looked
very cross and said: "This is my
beach! You must go away!"

"We certainly shan't," said
Moominmamma. "So there!" Then
the ant-lion began to kick sand in
her eyes, he kicked and scratched
until she could not see a thing. Closer and
closer he came, and suddenly he began to dig himself into
the sand, making the hole deeper and deeper around him. At
last only his eyes could be seen at the bottom of the hole, and
all the while he continued to throw sand at Moominmamma.

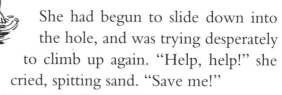

She had begun to slide down into the hole, and was trying desperately to climb up again. "Help, help!" she cried, spitting sand. "Save me!"

Moomintroll heard her and came rushing up out of the water. He managed to catch hold of her ears and pulled and struggled with all his might while he shouted rude names at the ant-lion. The little creature and Tulippa came and helped too, and then, at last, they managed to haul Moominmamma over the edge, and she was rescued. (The ant-lion continued to dig himself in out of pure annoyance, and no one knows if he ever found the way up again.) It was a long while until they got the sand out of their eyes and managed to calm down a little. But by then they had lost all their desire to swim, and instead continued along the seashore in order to look for a boat. The sun was already going down and behind the horizon, threatening black clouds were gathering. It looked as though there was going to be a storm. Suddenly they caught sight of something moving farther along the shore.

It was a mass of small, pale creatures, pushing out a sail-boat. Moominmamma looked at them for a long time, and then she called loudly: "Those are the wanderers! Those are the Hattifatteners!" and began to run towards them as fast as she could. By the time Moomintroll, the little creature, and Tulippa got there, Moominmamma was standing in the midst of the Hattifatteners (who only came up to her waist), talking and asking questions and waving her arms, very excitedly. She asked over and over again if they really had not seen Moominpappa, but the Hattifatteners only looked at her for a moment with their round, colourless eyes and then went on pulling the boat towards the water. "Oh dear," Moominmamma exclaimed, "I was in such a hurry that I forgot they can't speak or hear anything!" And she drew a handsome Moomintroll in the sand with a big question-mark after him. But the Hattifatteners did not bother about her at all, they had got the boat down into the sea and were busy hoisting the sails. (It is also possible that they did not understand what she meant, for Hattifatteners are very stupid.)

The black bank of cloud had now risen higher, and waves
were beginning to move on the sea.

"There's nothing for it, we shall have to go with them,"
said Moominmamma, at last. "The shore looks gloomy and
deserted, and I don't feel like meeting another ant-lion. Jump
into the boat, children!"

"Well, it's not on my head!" mumbled the little creature,
but he climbed on board after the others all the same. The
boat steered out to sea with a Hattifattener at the helm. The
sky grew darker and darker all around, the tops of the waves
had white foam on them, and far away thunder was rumbling.
As it fluttered in the gale, Tulippa's hair glowed with a very
faint light.

"Now I'm frightened again," said the little creature. "I'm almost beginning to wish I hadn't come with you at all."

"Pooh," said Moomintroll, but then he lost the desire to say any more and crept down beside his mother. Now and then came a wave that was bigger than all the others and splashed in over the bow. The boat sailed on with taut sails at a furious speed. Sometimes they saw a mermaid dance by on the crests of the waves, sometimes they glimpsed a whole flock of little sea-trolls. The thunder rumbled louder and the lightning ran crisscross over the sky. "Now I feel seasick, too," said the little creature, and then he was sick while Moominmamma held his head. The sun had set long ago, but in the gleam of the lightning they noticed a sea-troll that kept trying to keep abreast of the boat. "Hello there!" cried Moomintroll through the storm, to show that he was not afraid. "Hello, hello," said the sea-troll. "You look as though you might be a relation."

"That would be nice," cried Moomintroll, politely. (But he thought it was probably a very distant relation, because moomintrolls are a much finer species than sea-trolls.)

"Jump into the boat," Tulippa called to the sea-troll, "otherwise you'll be left behind!"

The sea-troll took a leap over the gunwale of the boat and shook the water off himself like a dog. "Grand weather," he said. "Where are you bound for?"

"Anywhere, as long as we can reach land," groaned the little creature, who was quite green in the face with seasickness.

"In that case I had better take the helm for a bit," said the sea-troll. "If you keep on this course, you'll go straight out to sea."

And then he took over from the Hattifattener who sat at the helm, and made the boat alter course. It was strange how much easier it was now that they had the sea-troll with them. The boat danced along, and sometimes it made long leaps over the peaks of the waves.

The little creature began to look more cheerful, and Moomintroll shrieked with delight. Only the Hattifatteners sat staring indifferently at the horizon. They did not care about anything except travelling on from one strange place to the other.

"I know a fine harbour," said the sea-troll. "But the entrance is so narrow that only superior seamen like myself can manage it." He laughed loudly and made the boat make a mighty leap over the waves. Then they saw land rising out of the sea under the forked lightning. Moominmamma thought it was a wild and creepy land. "Is there anything to eat there?" she asked.

"There's anything you like," said the sea-troll. "Hold on, for we're going to sail right into the harbour now!"

At that same moment the boat rushed into a black ravine where the storm howled between the enormously high faces

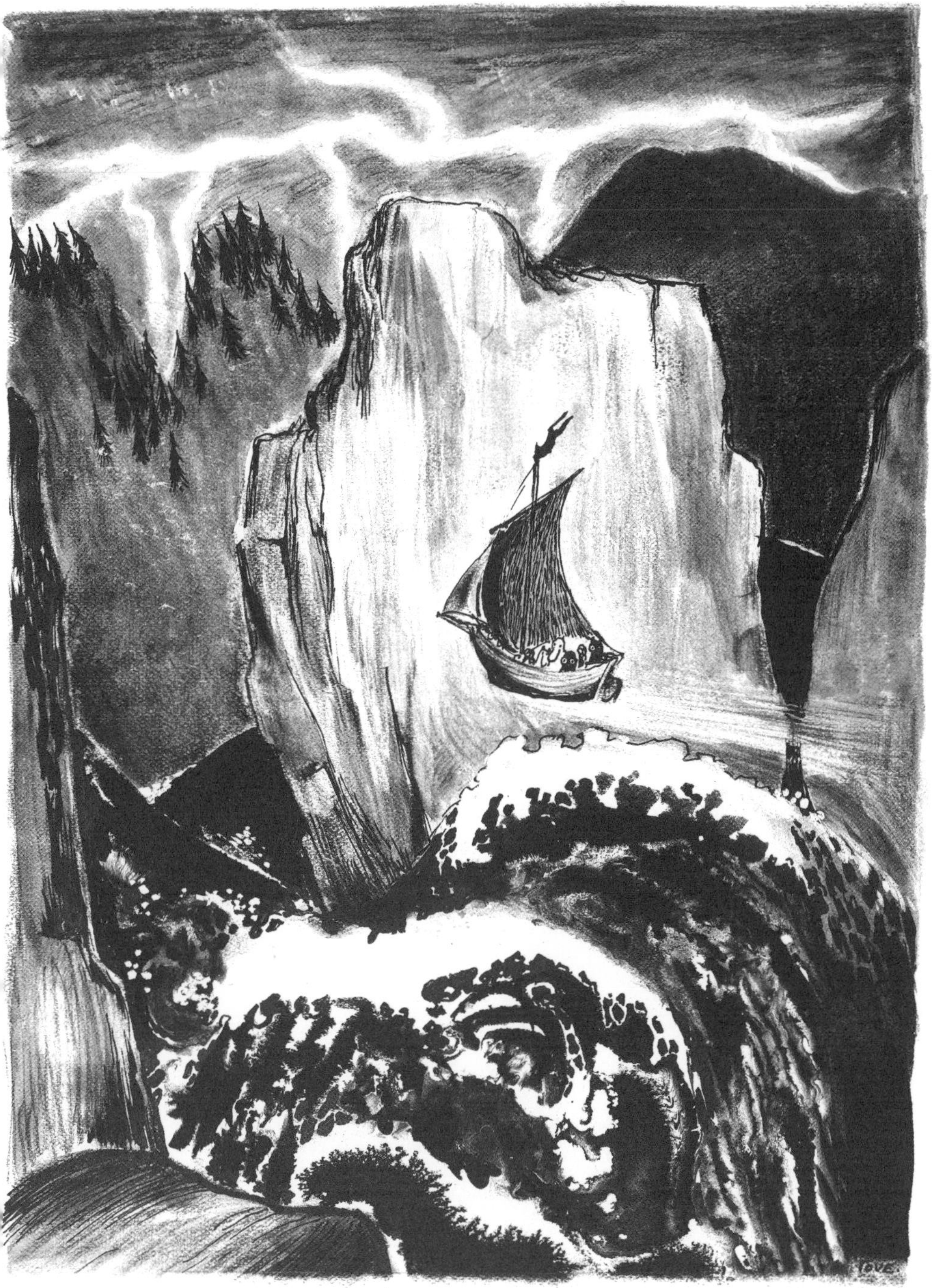
TOVE.

of rock. The sea foamed white against the cliffs and it looked as though the boat was plunging straight towards them. But it flew light as a bird into a large harbour where the transparent water was as calm and green as in a lagoon.

"Thank goodness," said Moominmamma, for she had not really trusted the sea-troll. "It does look nice here."

"It depends on your taste," said the sea-troll. "I suppose I prefer it when a storm is raging. I'd best be off before the waves get smaller." And then he somersaulted down into the sea, and was gone.

When the Hattifatteners saw an unknown land before them, they livened up; some began to furl the slack sails and others put out the oars and rowed eagerly towards the flowering green shore. The boat put in at a meadow that was full of wild flowers, and Moomintroll jumped ashore with the mooring rope.

"Now bow and thank the Hattifatteners for the voyage," said Moominmamma. And Moomintroll made a deep bow, and the little creature wagged his tail gratefully.

"Thank you very much," said Moominmamma and Tulippa, and they curtseyed down to the ground. But when they all looked up again, the Hattifatteners had gone on their way.

"I expect they made themselves invisible," said the little creature. "Funny folk."

Then all four of them went in among the flowers. The sun was rising now, and the dew was glittering and gleaming.

"This is where I'd like to live," said Tulippa. "These flowers are even more beautiful than my old tulip. Besides, my hair never really matched it properly."

"Look, a house made of real gold!" shouted the little creature suddenly, pointing. In the middle of the meadow stood a tower with the sun reflecting itself in its long row of windows. The top storey was made entirely of glass, and the sunlight gleamed in it like burning red gold.

"I wonder who lives there," said Moominmamma. "Perhaps it's too early to wake them."

"But I'm so horribly hungry," said Moomintroll. "Me too," said the little creature and Tulippa.

And then they all looked at Moominmamma. "Well—all right, then," she said, and then she went up to the tower and knocked on the door.

After a little while, a hatch in the door opened and a boy with completely red hair looked out. "Are you shipwrecked?" he asked.

"Almost," said Moominmamma. "But we're most definitely hungry."

Then the boy opened the door wide and invited them to come in. And when he caught sight of Tulippa, he made a deep bow, for he had never seen such beautiful blue hair before. And Tulippa curtseyed just as deeply, for she thought his red hair was absolutely lovely. Then they all followed him up the spiral staircase, all the way to the top storey made of glass, where they could see out over the sea in all directions. In the midst of the tower room was a table on which there was an enormous bowl of steaming sea pudding.

"Is that really for us?" asked Moominmamma.

"Of course," said the boy. "I keep a lookout here when there's a storm out at sea, and all who escape into my harbour are invited for sea pudding. That's how it's always been."

Then they sat round the table and after a very short while, the whole basin was empty. (The little creature, who sometimes did not have very good manners, took the bowl with him under the table and licked it completely clean.)

"Thank you so awfully much," said Moominmamma. "You must have invited quite a lot of people up here for sea pudding, I should think."

"Oh yes," said the boy. "People from every corner of the world. Snufkins, Sea-ghosts, Little Creeps and Big Folk, Snorks and Hemulens. And the odd angler fish, too."

"I suppose you haven't seen any moomins, by any chance?" asked Moominmmma, and she was so excited that her voice quivered.

"Yes, one," said the boy. "That was after the cyclone last Monday."

"That couldn't have been Moominpappa, could it?" cried Moomintroll. "Did he keep putting his tail in his pocket?"

"Yes, he did, actually," said the boy. "I remember it quite particularly, because it looked so funny."

Then Moomintroll and his mother were so happy that they fell into each other's arms, and the little creature jumped up and down and cried "hurrah."

"Where did he go?" asked Moominmamma. "Did he say anything particular? Where is he? How was he?"

"Fine," said the boy. "He took the road to the south."

"Then we must go after him at once," said Moominmamma. "Perhaps we'll catch up with him. Hurry up, children. Where's my handbag?" And then she rushed down the spiral staircase so fast that they could scarcely follow her.

"Wait!" cried the boy. "Wait a bit!" He caught up with them in the doorway.

"You must forgive us for not saying goodbye properly," said Moominmamma, who was hopping up and down with impatience. "But you see…"

"It's not that," said the boy, now as red in the face as his hair. I just thought—I mean whether by any chance…"

"Well, out with it," said Moominmamma.

"Tulippa," said the boy. "Fair Tulippa, I suppose you wouldn't like to stay with me, would you?"

"Gladly," replied Tulippa at once, looking happy. "All the time I was sitting up there, I was thinking how well my hair might shine for seafarers in your glass tower. And I'm very good at making sea pudding." But then she became a little anxious, and looked at Moominmamma. "Of course I would terribly like to help you to look as well…" she said.

"Oh, I'm sure we'll manage," said Moominmamma. "We'll send you both a letter and tell you what happens."

Then they all hugged one another goodbye and Moomintroll went on his way southwards with his mother and the little creature. All day they walked through the flowering landscape, which Moomintroll would have liked to explore on his own. But his mother was in a hurry and would not let him stop. "Have you ever seen such funny trees?" asked the little creature. "With such terribly long trunks and then a little tuft at the top. I think they look silly."

"It's you who's silly," said Moominmamma, who was on edge. "Actually, they're palm trees and they always look like that."

"Have it your own way!" said the little creature, who was offended.

It had become very hot late in the afternoon. Everywhere the plants drooped, and the sun shone down with a creepy red light. Even though Moomins are very fond of warmth, they felt quite limp

and would have liked to rest under one of the large cactuses that grew everywhere. But Moominmamma could not rest until they had found some trace of Moomintroll's Papa. They continued on their way straight southwards, even though it was already beginning to get dark.

Suddenly the little creature stopped and listened. "What's that pattering around us?" he asked.

And now they could hear a whispering and a rustling among the leaves. "It's only the rain," said Moominmamma. "Now we must crawl in under the cactuses anyway."

All night it rained, and in the morning it was simply pouring down in bucketfuls. When they looked out, everything was grey and melancholy.

"It's no good, we must go on," said Moominmamma. "But here is something for you that I've been saving until it was really needed." And then she produced a large bar of chocolate from her handbag. She had taken it with her from the old gentleman's wonderful garden. She split it in two and gave them each a piece.

"Aren't you going to have some?" asked Moomintroll.

"No," said his mother. "I don't like chocolate."

So they walked on in the pouring rain all that day and all the next day, too. All they found to eat were a few sopping wet yams and one or two figs.

On the third day it rained harder than ever and each little rivulet had become a foaming torrent. It became more and more difficult to make any progress, the water rose ceaselessly, and at last they had to climb up on to a small rock so as not to be snatched away by the current. There they sat, watching the rushing eddies come closer and closer to them, and feeling that they were catching cold. Floating around everywhere were furniture and houses and big trees that the flood had carried with it.

"I think I want to go home!" said the little creature, but no one listened to him. The others had caught sight of something strange that was dancing and whirling towards them in the water.

"They've been shipwrecked!" cried Moomintroll, who had sharp eyes. "A whole family! Mamma, we must rescue them!"

The thing that was lurching towards them was an upholstered armchair; sometimes it got caught in the treetops that stuck up out of the water, but was pulled free by the current and went drifting on. In the chair sat a wet cat with five equally wet kittens around her.

"Poor mother!" cried Moominmamma, and she jumped out into the water all the way up to her waist. "Hold on to me, and I'll try to catch them with my tail!"

Moomintroll took a steady hold of his mother, and the little creature was so excited that it did not manage to do anything at all. Now the armchair was whirling by; like lightning Moominmamma tied her tail in a half hitch round one of the armrests, and then she pulled.

"Heave-ho!" she cried.

"Heave-ho!" cried Moomintroll.

"Ho, ho!" squeaked the little creature. "Don't let go!"

Slowly the chair swung in towards the rock, and then a helpful wave came and took it up on to the land. The cat picked up her kittens by the scruff of their necks, one by one, and put them in a row to dry.

"Thank you for your kind help," she said. "This is the worst thing that has ever happened to me. It was a cat-astrophe!"

And then she began to lick her children.

"I think the weather's clearing up," said the little creature, who wanted to make them think about something else. (He was embarrassed because he had not managed to help in the rescue.) And it was true—the clouds were moving apart and a shaft of sunlight flew straight down, and then another—and all of a sudden the sun was shining over the enormous, steaming surface of the water.

"Hurrah!" cried Moomintroll. "Now everything will be all right, you'll see!"

A small breeze arose and chased the clouds away and shook the treetops that were heavy with rain. The agitated water calmed down, somewhere a bird began to chirp, and the cat purred in the sunshine. "Now we can go on," said Moominmamma firmly."We don't have time to wait until the water sinks away. Get up into the armchair, children, and then I'll push it out into the lake."

"I shall stay here," said the cat, and yawned. "One should never make a needless fuss. When the ground is dry I'll walk home again." And her five kittens, who had recovered in the sunshine, sat up and yawned too.

Then Moominmamma pushed the armchair out from the shore. "Go carefully!" cried the little creature. He was sitting on the backrest and looking around, for it had occurred to him that they might find something valuable floating in the water after the flood. For example, a casket full of jewels. Why not? He kept a sharp watch, and when he suddenly saw something gleaming in the water, he shouted loudly with excitement. "Go that way," he cried. "There's something shining over there!"

"We haven't got time to fish up everything that's floating around," said Moominmamma, but she paddled that way all the same, because she was a kind mamma.

"It's just an old bottle," said the little creature, disappointed, when he had hauled it up with his tail.

"And no nice sweet drink in it either," said Moomintroll.

"But don't you see?" said his mother seriously. "It's something very interesting, it's a message in a bottle. There's a letter inside." And then she took a corkscrew out of her handbag and uncorked the bottle.

With trembling hands she spread out the letter on her knee and read aloud:

Dear finder, please do what you can to rescue me! My beautiful house has been swept away by the flood and now I am sitting lonely, hungry, and cold in a tree while the water rises higher and higher.

An unhappy moomin

"Lonely and hungry and cold," said Moominmamma, and she cried. "Oh, my poor dear Moomintroll, your father has probably drowned long ago!"

"Don't cry," said Moomintroll. "Perhaps he's sitting in a tree somewhere very close. After all, the water is going down as fast as can be." And so it was.

Here and there, hillocks and fences and roofs were already sticking up above the surface of the water, and now the birds were singing at the tops of their voices.

The armchair bobbed slowly along towards a hill where a lot of people were running about, pulling their belongings out of the water. "Why, there's my armchair," cried a big Hemulen who was gathering his dining room furniture together on the shore.

"What do you think you're doing sailing around in my armchair?"

"And a rotten boat it made, too!" said Moominmamma, crossly, and she stepped ashore. "I wouldn't have it for anything in the world!"

"Don't annoy him," whispered the little creature. "He may bite!"

"Rubbish," said Moominmamma. "Come along now, children." And they walked along the shore, while the Hemulen examined the wet stuffing in his chair.

"Look!" said Moomintroll, pointing to a marabou stork who was walking around, scolding to himself. "I wonder what he's lost—he looks even angrier than the Hemulen!"

"Little impudent child," said the marabou stork, for he had good ears. "If you were nearly a hundred years old and had lost your spectacles, you wouldn't look exactly pleased, either." And then he turned his back to them and continued his search.

"Come along now," said Moominmamma. "We must look for your father."

She took Moomintroll and the little creature by the hand and hurried on. After a while they saw something gleaming in the grass where the water had subsided. "I bet it's a diamond!" cried the little creature. But when they looked more closely, they saw that it was only a pair of spectacles.

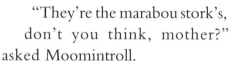

"They're the marabou stork's, don't you think, mother?" asked Moomintroll.

"Must be," she said. "You had better run back and give them to him. But hurry up, for your poor father is sitting somewhere hungry and wet and all alone."

Moomintroll ran as fast as he could on his short legs, until in the distance he saw the stork poking about in the water. "Hello there, hello!" he cried. "Here are your spectacles, Uncle Stork!"

"Well, fancy that!" said the marabou stork, very pleased. "Perhaps you are not such an impossible little child after all." And then he put on his spectacles and turned his head this way and that.

"I really must go at once," said Moomintroll. "You see, we're searching too."

"Well, well, I see," said the marabou stork in a friendly voice. "What for?"

"My father," said Moomintroll. "He's up a tree somewhere."

The marabou stork thought for a long time. Then he said firmly: "You will never manage it alone. But I will help you, because you found my spectacles."

Then he picked up Moomintroll in his beak, very carefully, and put him on his back, flapped his wings a few times, and sailed away over the shore.

Moomintroll had never flown before, and he thought it was tremendous fun, and a little scary. He was also quite proud when the marabou stork landed beside his mother and the little creature.

"I am at your service in the matter of searches, madam," said

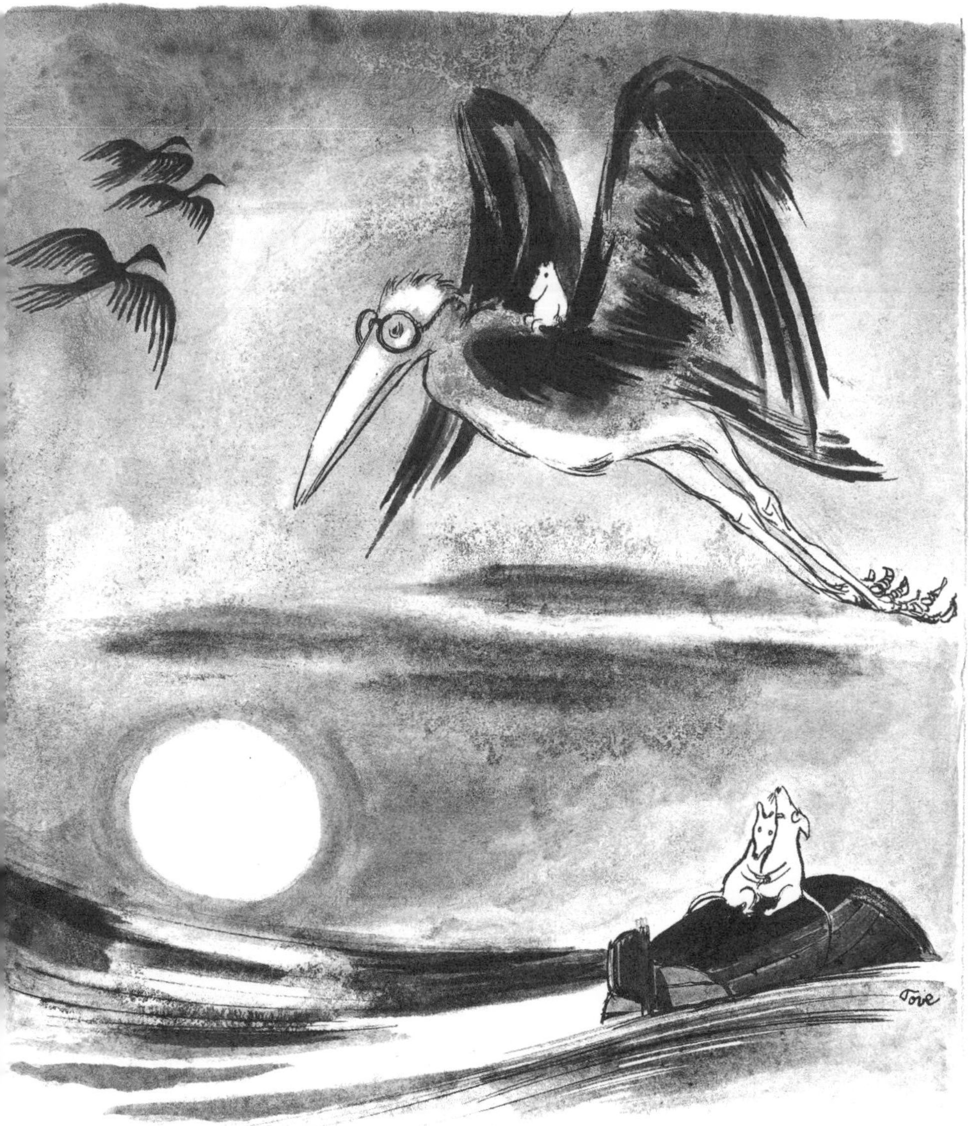
Tove

the marabou stork, bowing to Moominmamma. "If the family will climb on board we shall effect our departure at once." And then he lifted first her and then the little creature, who squeaked with excitement. "Hold on tight," he said. "We're going to fly out over the water now."

"I think this is the most wonderful thing we've been through so far," said Moominmamma. "Why, flying is not nearly as frightening as I thought. Now keep a good look out for Moominpappa in all directions!"

The marabou stork flew in wide circles and came in low over each treetop. They saw a lot of people sitting amidst the branches, but none of them was who they were looking for. "I shall have to rescue those Creeps over there later on," said the marabou stork, who had become really inspired by the rescue expedition. He flew to and fro above the water for a long time, the sun began to set and then everything seemed quite hopeless.

Suddenly Moominmamma cried: "There he is!" and began to wave her arms so wildly that she nearly fell off.

"Papa!" shouted Moomintroll, and the little creature cried out too, out of pure sympathy.

There, on one of the highest branches of an enormous tree sat a wet, sad Moominpappa, staring out over the water. Beside him he had tied a distress flag. He was so amazed and delighted when the marabou stork landed in the tree and the whole of his family climbed down onto the branches that he could not say a word. "Now we shall never be separated again," sniffed Moominmamma, and took him in her arms. "How are you? Have you caught cold? Where have you been all this time? Was the house you built a very fine one? Did you think of us often?"

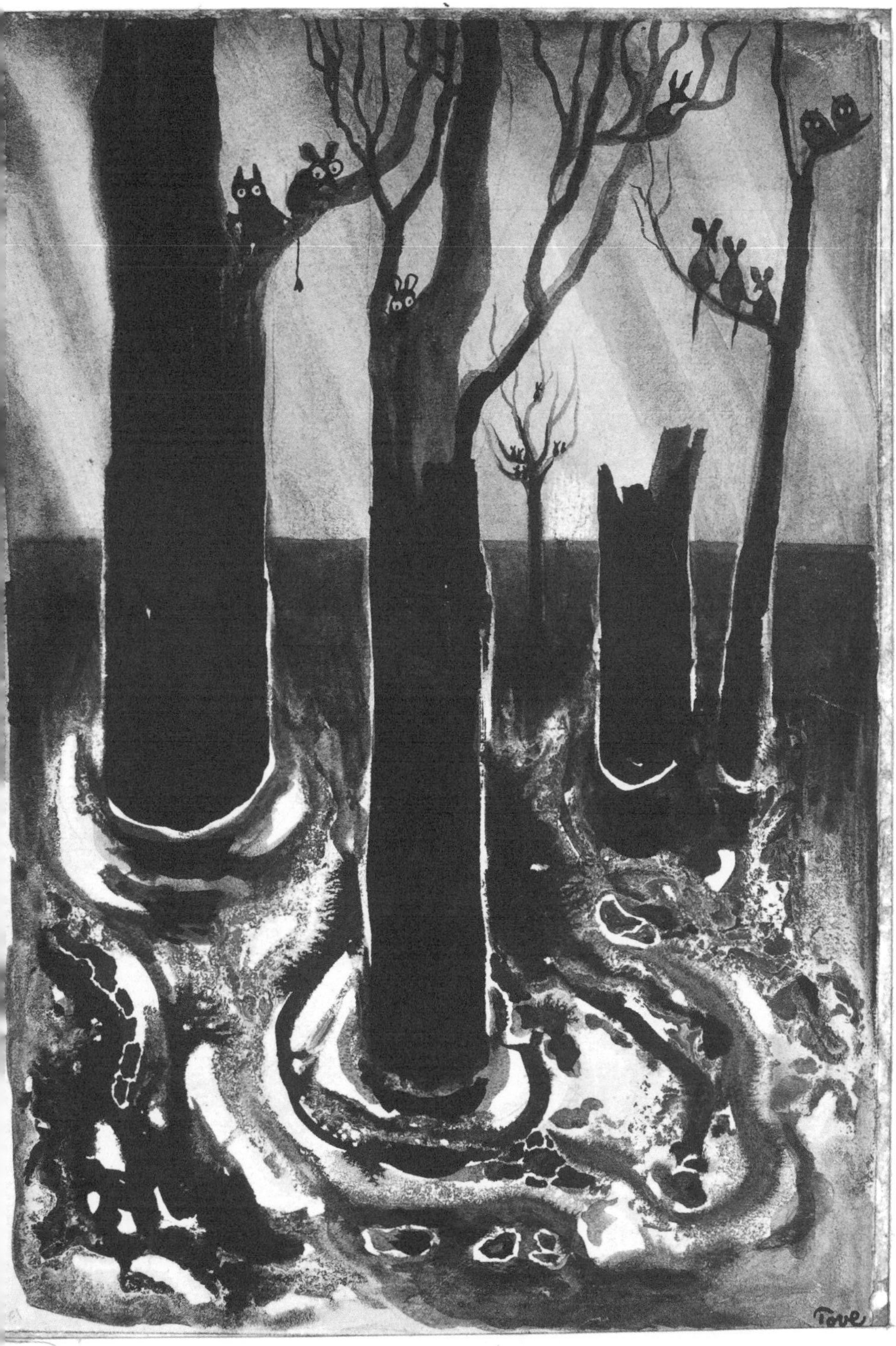
Tove

"It was a very fine house, alas," said Moominpappa. "My dear little boy, how you have grown!"

"Well, well," said the marabou stork, who was beginning to feel touched. "I think I had better put you down on dry land and try to rescue a few more before the sun goes down. It's very pleasant, rescuing people." And then he took them back to the shore while they all talked at the same time about every dreadful thing they had been through. All along the shore people had lit fires at which they were warming themselves and cooking food, for most had lost their homes. The marabou stork put down Moomintroll, his father and mother, and the little creature at one of the bonfires, and with a hasty farewell he flew out over the water again.

"Good evening," said the two angler fish who had lit the fire. "Do sit down, the soup will be ready in a moment."

"Thank you very much," said Moominpappa. "You have no idea what a fine house I had before the flood. Built it all by myself. But if I get a new one, you will be welcome any time."

"How big was it?" asked the little creature.

"Three rooms," said Moominpappa. "One sky-blue, one sunshine-yellow, and one spotted. And a guest room in the attic for you, little creature."

"Did you really mean us to live there too?" asked Moominmamma, very pleased.

"Of course," he said. "I looked for you always, everywhere. I could never forget our dear old stove."

Then they sat and told one another about their experiences and ate soup until the moon had risen and the fires began to go out along the shore. Then they borrowed a blanket from

the angler fish and curled up close next to one another and fell asleep.

By morning the water had gone down a good way, and they all went out into the sunshine in a very good mood. The little creature danced in front of them and tied a bow in his tail because he was so happy. All day they walked, and wherever they went it was beautiful, for after the rain the most wonderful flowers had come out everywhere and the trees had both flowers and fruit. They only needed to shake a tree slightly, and the fruit fell down around them.

At last they came to a small valley that was more beautiful than any they had seen that day. And there, in the midst of the meadow, stood a house that almost looked like a tall stove, very elegant and painted blue. "Why, that's my house!" cried Moominpappa, quite beside himself with joy. "It must have floated here, and here it is!"

"Hurrah!" shouted the little creature, and then they all rushed down into the valley to admire the house. The little creature even climbed up on the roof, and there he shouted even louder, for up on the chimney hung a necklace of large, real pearls that had lodged there during the flood.

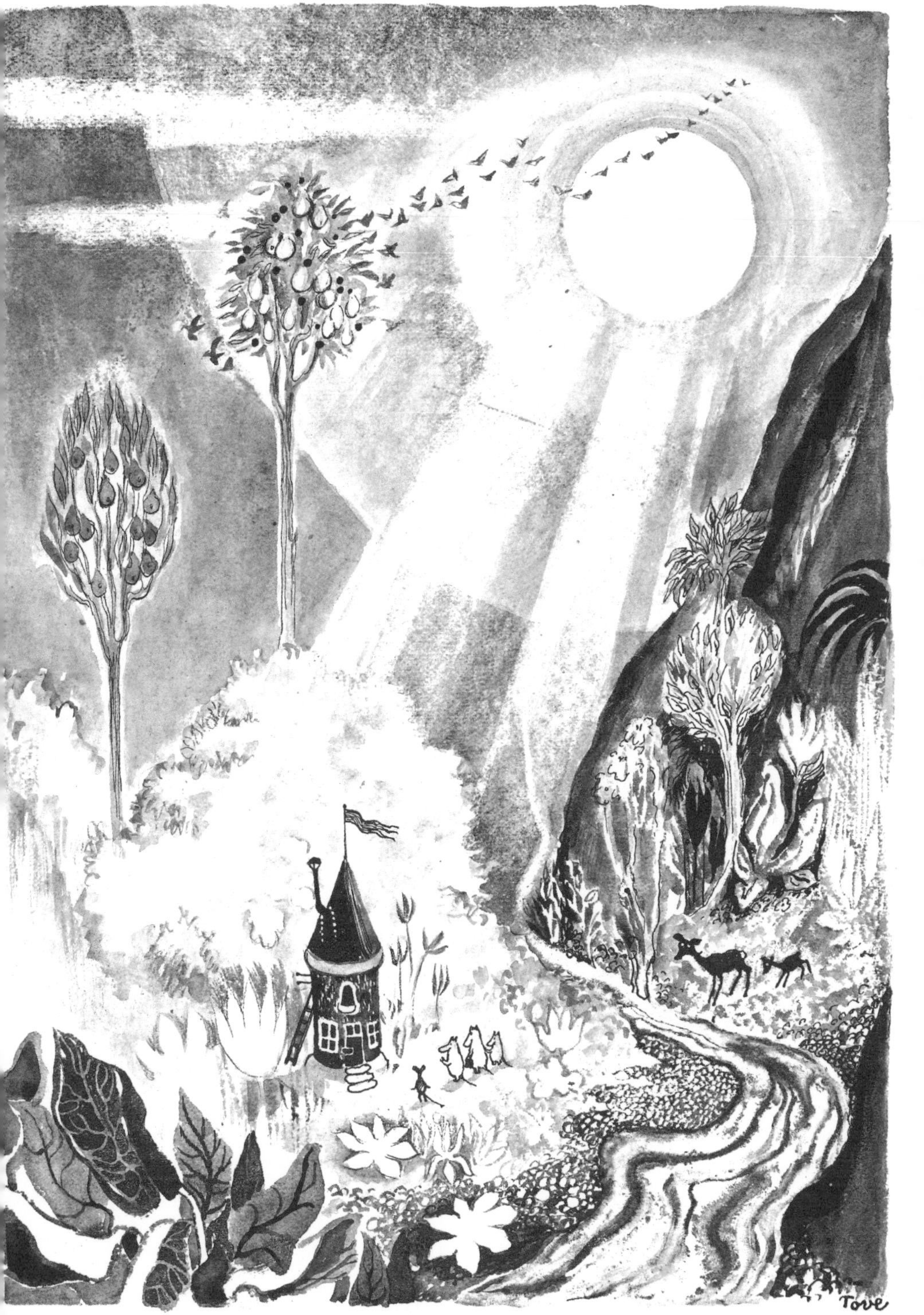
Tove

"Now we are rich!" he cried. "We can buy a car and an even bigger house!"

"No," said Moominmamma. "This house is the most beautiful one we could ever have."

And then she took Moomintroll by the hand and went into the sky-blue room. And there in the valley they spent the whole of their lives, apart from a few times when they left it and travelled for a change.

TOVE JANSSON
(1914–2001)

TOVE JANSSON is Scandinavia's best-known and best-loved children's author. She began publishing sketches and cartoons at the age of fifteen and was already a respected artist when her first book, *The Moomins and the Great Flood*, was published in 1945. This book introduced an early version of Moomintroll and the characters for which she would become internationally renowned. Tove Jansson lived in Helsinki but spent a large part of her life on an island in the Gulf of Finland.

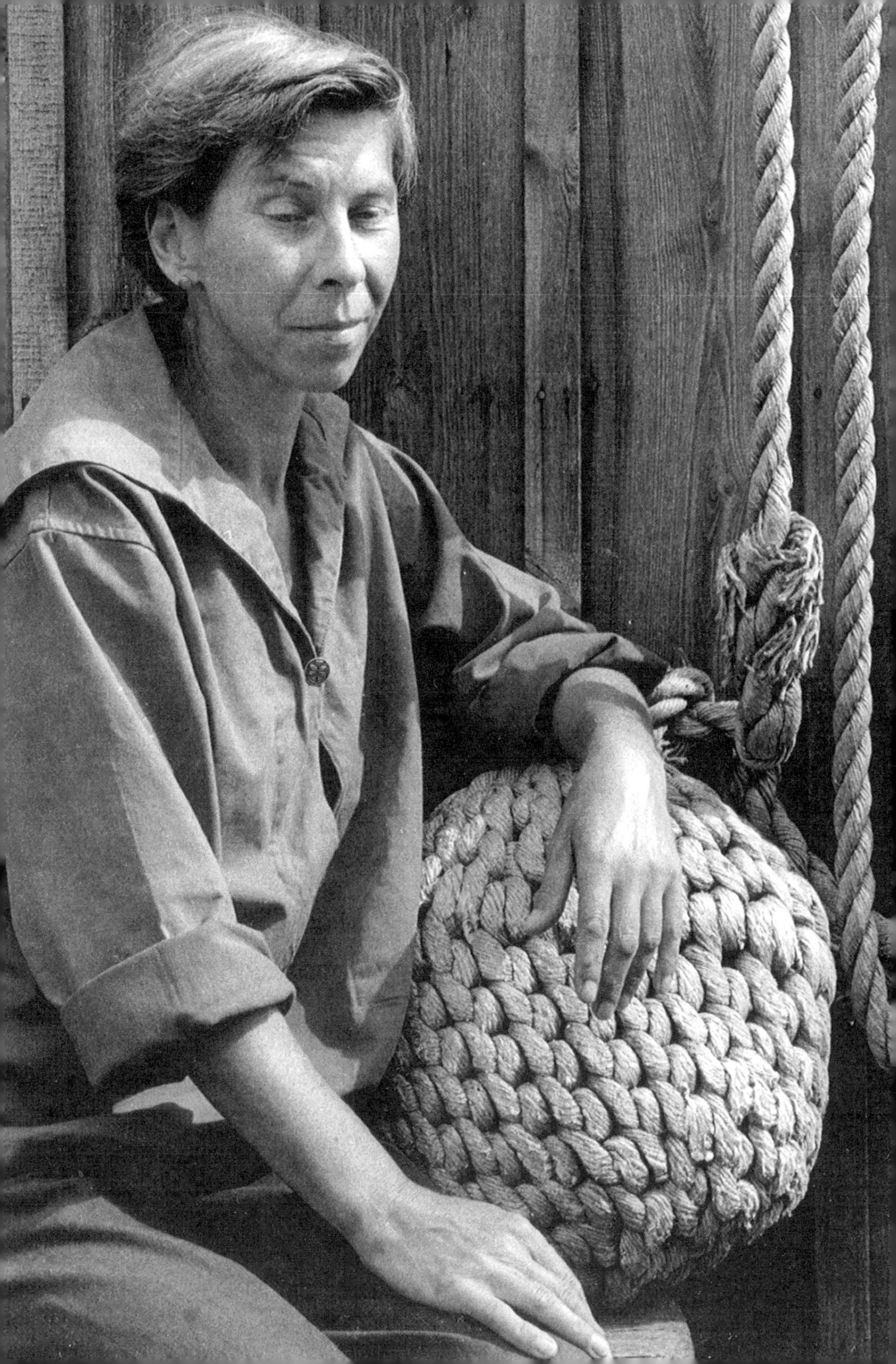

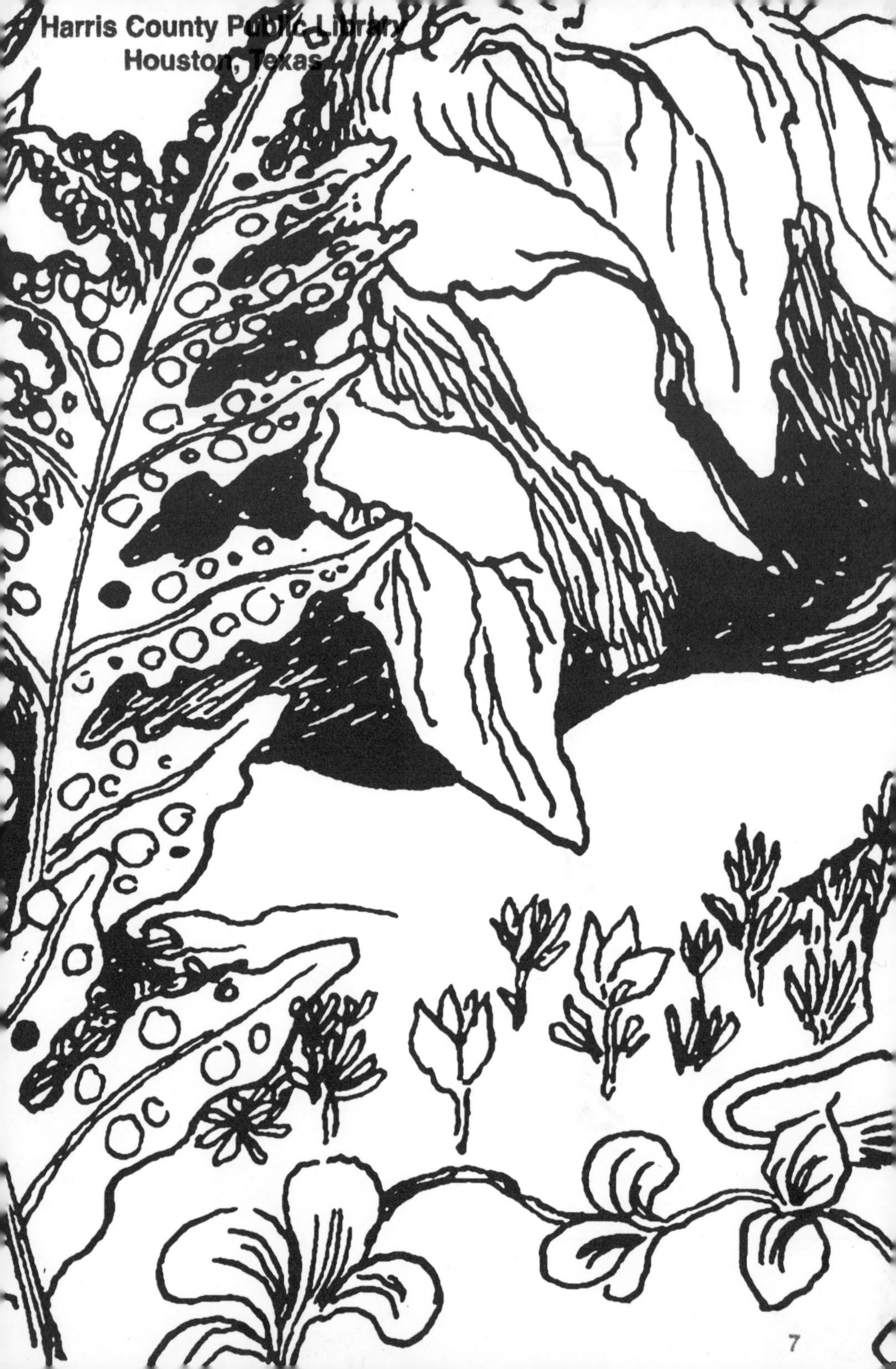